JE NEI

Neitzel, Shirley.

I'm taking a trip on my
 train /
             9/49 ANGELOU

6x 1/00 4/00
6x 9/01 LT 2/00

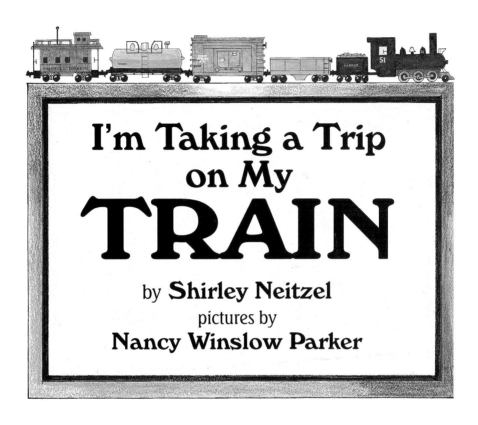

I'm Taking a Trip on My TRAIN

by **Shirley Neitzel**

pictures by
Nancy Winslow Parker

Greenwillow Books New York

For Jeffrey, the engineer,
and his crew, Scott and Dana
—S. N.

For Mary Ann, Tom, Bruce,
Blaine, Ridgely, and Peter
—N. W. P.

The model railroad I have drawn is
the No. 1 scale model. In this scale,
a 41-foot boxcar is 15 1/2 inches long,
3 5/8 inches wide, and 5 1/2 inches high.
—N. W. P.

Watercolor paints, colored pencils, and a black
pen were used to prepare the full-color art.
The text type is Seagull Light BT.

Text copyright © 1999 by Shirley Neitzel
Illustrations copyright © 1999
by Nancy Winslow Parker

Printed in Hong Kong by South China Printing
Company (1988) Ltd.
First Edition   10 9 8 7 6 5 4 3 2 1

Library of Congress Cataloging-in-Publication Data
Neitzel, Shirley.
I'm taking a trip on my train / by Shirley Neitzel;
pictures by Nancy Winslow Parker.
          p.   cm.
Summary: In cumulative verses using rebuses,
a young boy describes his experiences as engineer
on the train in his room.
ISBN 0-688-15833-1 (trade)
ISBN 0-688-15834-X (lib. bdg.)
1. Rebuses   [1. Railroads—Trains—Fiction.
2. Imagination—Fiction.   3. Stories in rhyme.
4. Rebuses.]   I. Parker, Nancy Winslow, ill.
II.Title.   PZ8.3.N341m   1999
[E]—dc21   98-2979   CIP   AC

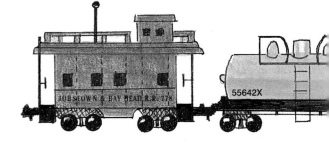

I'm taking a trip on my train.

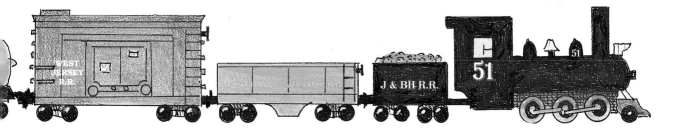

When I wear my striped cap,

I'm the engineer,

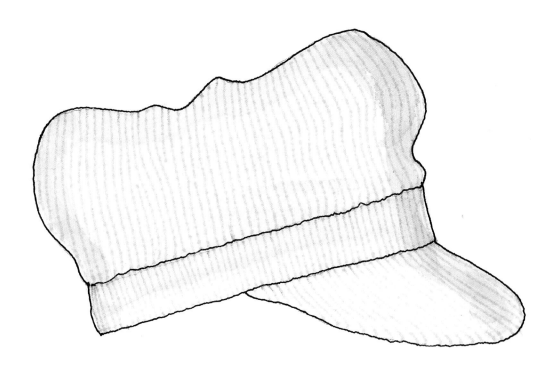

and I'm taking a trip on my

A bright red caboose

is at the rear.

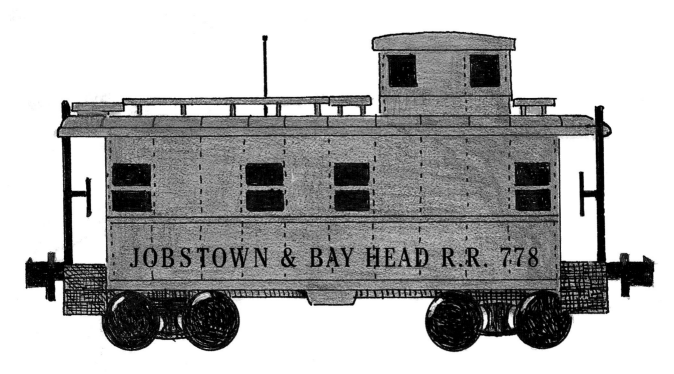

When I wear my striped I'm the engineer,

and I'm taking a trip on my

Here's my locomotive—
it's shiny and black,

and a bright red  is at the rear.

When I wear my striped I'm the engineer,

and I'm taking a trip on my

I'll wave to the people
along the track

from my  shiny and black,

and a bright red  is at the rear.

When I wear my striped I'm the engineer,

and I'm taking a trip on my

There are gondolas and boxcars

(with doors that slide),

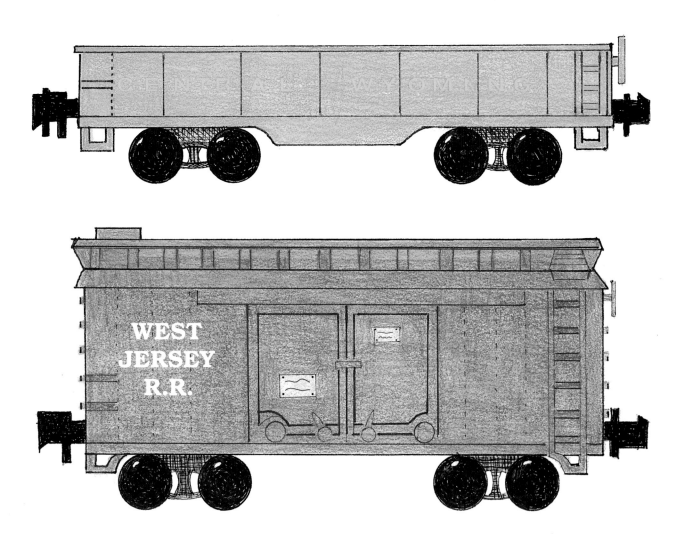

and I'll wave to the  along the track

from my 51 shiny and black,

and a bright red is at the rear.

When I wear my striped I'm the engineer,

and I'm taking a trip on my

I have long, round tankers

(with liquid inside),

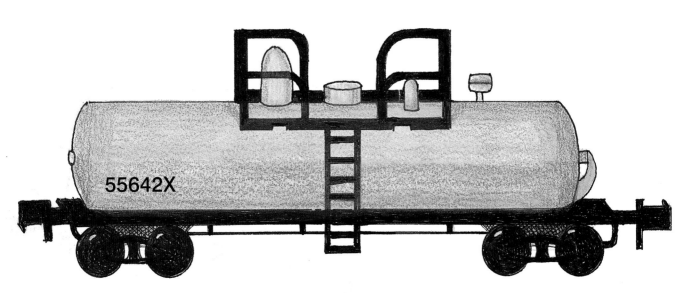

55642X

and ___ and ___ (with doors that slide),

and I'll wave to the ___ along the track

from my ___ shiny and black,

and a bright red ___ is at the rear.

When I wear my striped ___ I'm the engineer,

and I'm taking a trip on my

I'll go over a trestle

that's high in the air,

pulling long, round 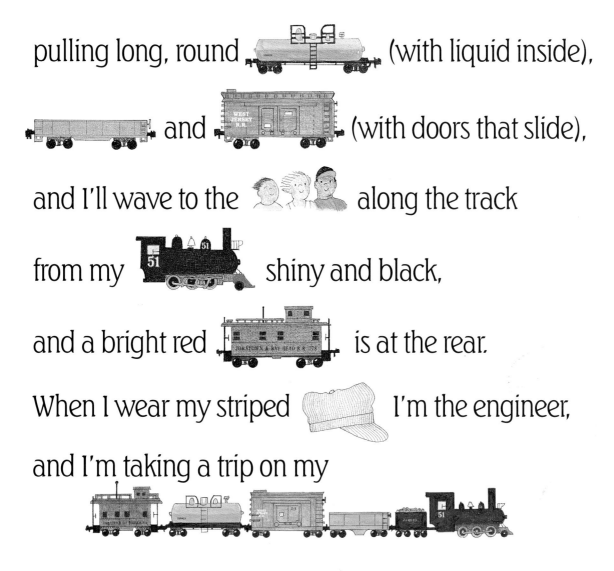 (with liquid inside),

and (with doors that slide),

and I'll wave to the along the track

from my shiny and black,

and a bright red is at the rear.

When I wear my striped I'm the engineer,

and I'm taking a trip on my

I'll zip through the tunnel

(it's dark in there)

and go over a 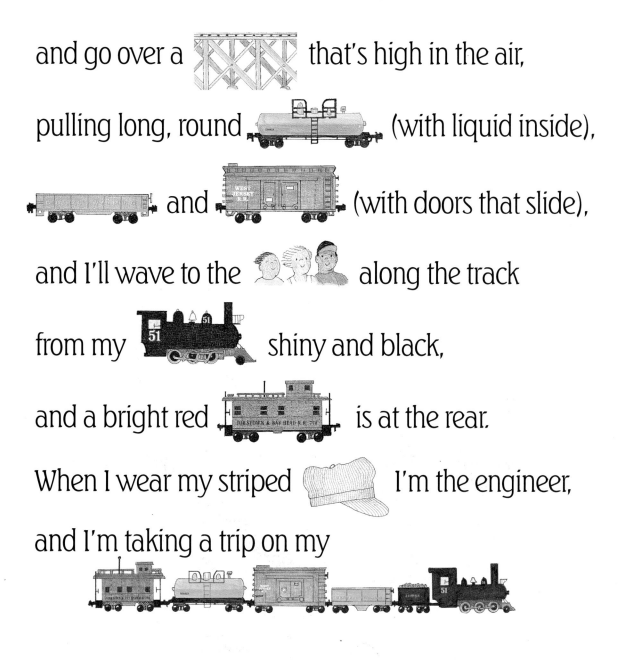 that's high in the air,

pulling long, round (with liquid inside),

 and (with doors that slide),

and I'll wave to the along the track

from my shiny and black,

and a bright red is at the rear.

When I wear my striped I'm the engineer,

and I'm taking a trip on my

I'll check my watch,

so I won't be late,

as I zip through the (it's dark in there)

and go over a that's high in the air,

pulling long, round (with liquid inside),

and (with doors that slide),

and I'll wave to the along the track

from my shiny and black,

and a bright red is at the rear.

When I wear my striped I'm the engineer,

and I'm taking a trip on my

The whistle
will sound
at the signal
and gate,

then I'll check my  so I won't be late,

as I zip through the (it's dark in there)

and go over a that's high in the air,

pulling long, round (with liquid inside),

and (with doors that slide),

and I'll wave to the along the track

from my shiny and black,

and a bright red is at the rear.

When I wear my striped I'm the engineer,

and I'm taking a trip on my

Then Mother walked in and said, "It's clear

from your cap and your watch,
you're the engineer.

"And you've made your sister into a star

by letting her whistle and count every car.

"You've traveled, no doubt, to far-away places,

seen rivers and mountains and many new faces.

"I have a request (I don't think it's too hard):
Before going to bed, pick up this freight yard,

"because during the night I'd like to refrain
from taking an unplanned trip on your train."